Manfred Gottert

Wow! You see! Definitely: Chickenpox!

Father and Son.
Often a complicated
relationship.
Especially in the
beginning.

Bibliografische Information
der Deutschen Nationalbibliothek:
Die Deutsche Nationalbibliothek verzeichnet diese
Publikation in der Deutschen Nationalbibliografie;
detaillierte bibliografische Daten sind im Internet
über dnb.dnb.de abrufbar.

1st edition

German title released in 2020:
"Krass! Siehst du! Eindeutig: Windpocken!"

Production and publishing:
BoD – Books on Demand, Norderstedt

ISBN: 9783754347744

Typesetting: Steffen Linke
Editing: Julie Köhler
Reviewing: Pia Yvonne Zang
Translation: Lara von Dehn
Podcast-Reading: Lukas Viernickel

For Finn and Maunzerle,
and especially for Susanne.

Chapter 1

There we are, or rather, there I am, standing outside the practice's door on the second floor, carrying Finn, his nursing bottle, and Mrs. Hansen. In front of us a sign: "Dear patients, everything gets stolen around here. Please lock your stroller and take your valuables with you to the practice."

Right. Daunted, we turn around and begin the descent without any remark on our part – no, not quite; Finn is blubbering, "Mommy-Mommy."

Back at the stroller, I notice the nursing bottle on the ground in front of us. Did we actually have two? Is that one even ours? But where is the other one, then? I stoop down to pick up the bottle as well as the bunting bag from the stroller. Finn tries to take advantage of this daring endeavor by tensing up all the muscles of his short, compact body to wield the light switch in the stairwell.

After gathering all utensils and locking the stroller and my bike, we start the second attempt, now holding Finn, the nursing bottle, the bulky bunting bag, my overstuffed backpack, and Mrs. Hansen.

Just when I got through the door at work today, Heike called. The first name 'Heike' is not very fitting; it should be 'Renate' maybe 'Elvira'. Definitely not Heike. She's too skinny and moody for this name, and her hairstyle is so inconspicuous that I can never seem to remember it at all.

Only the glasses. Yes, the glasses, I remember them: Once, VW Polo had a model named Harlekin, and it had differently colored parts. Whenever I see those glasses, I always wonder how many people bought this Volkswagen model and how many of these people were nurses and childcare workers. This style of glasses screams: Why not try something else sometimes?

But I was insistently told not to mess with people like that – it would harm the child. But I had to anyway – in the last three months, I secretly did it twice. The word 'kindergarten' is obviously lovely – 'educational institution', on the other hand, is not as appropriate. But Heike still doesn't like to be called a kindergarten teacher.

"YOUR SON HAS CHICKENPOX!!!"

Why on earth is it the case that the species of parents actually get called by their first name all the time?

Everyone. The kindergarten teachers, the other parents, the midwife, the receptionist. Every single one of them. At the age of 44, I'm really over people addressing me with the informal German term 'Du'. I wonder if the person, who sold Heike her glasses, also addressed her with 'Du' while they were softly whispering "pretty and playful" and "so sweet."

Hard to imagine.

On my bicycle, I dart from Prenzlauer Berg to Kreuzberg. I've got to eyeball the poor child together with snippy Heike, chubby Jasmin, and still another employee: "Look here. This one! See!! I'm sure of it, and he has a fever too – 37.7 degrees Celsius."

This is not the time for confronting her, but 37.7 degrees Celsius is the run-of-the-mill body temperature for this child. Does she not know his sweaty feet and this habit of doing all at the same time that he got from his mother?

That requires a bit more speed and fundamental energy. "Did he eat anything?" I ask concernedly.

"You bet; he was insatiable," Heike replies determinedly. Well, the usual then, I think, except for one or two little poxes. Without saying anything else, I wrap him up – tights, shirt, shoes, jacket – while Finn keeps trying to either poke out my eyes out or to just check the closing mechanism of my eyelids.

Petra, a receptionist I know very well from the crying therapy, calls to ask me to leave the child in the special cabins outside of the actual practice to quickly come to the registration without Finn.

When we open the practice door, we see a tube-like room with four glass cubicles measuring about one square meter each. Somehow, I get the impression that the pediatric practice has seen better days. The late '70s charm still shining through several layers of repainting cannot be denied. That's undoubtedly due to the effects of the health care crisis. At the end of the tube is a small window overlooking Hermannplatz and Karstadt. Otherwise, there is only the entrance door and the door to the registration desk.

I pick – no, Finn picks the first cabin. While the interior is relatively simple, rather reduced, the pressure inside the cabin is quite unpleasant. There is an exhaust system on the ceiling, possibly to catch Finn's toxic components right away. Next to it, only one of four halogen spotlights is glowing. But why it is so hot in this box is a mystery to me: To be able to undress without shivering with goosebumps? To provide the cell cultures with the best possible breeding ground? Or just to make the children particularly cranky? Half of the cabin is a maybe 1-meter-high platform coated with a worn plastic cover. Apart from that, there is only room for precisely one stool.

Finn's patience is already going downhill, and he would prefer to leave, same as I.

Chickenpox is not only an illness, but it also means that I won't be able to go to work again. Susanne has to see her patients, who can't be canceled at such short notice. I, on the other hand, tend to have a recession.

I wonder how other late-bearing self-employed people do it. In my case, there is an inversely proportional relationship between Finn's age and the net profit to be earned. In medical terms, you call that antagonistic when referring to muscles; it may be good for the muscles, but not so much for my general well-being.

I am convinced that the findings of the three pedagogical cognoscenti are correct. However, I would not necessarily exclude rabies as a diagnosis based on the symptoms, such as biting fits and a foaming mouth – or intolerance to his parents.

I put Finn on the worn plastic cover, take off my coat first, then his, and look for food and something to drink in the backpack. Somehow Finn gets off balance and falls to the ground.

Because I have no eyes in the back of my head, I can either get something from the backpack or stop him from suicidal activities. He screams. He decides to walk away without shoes and without permission.

I have to stop him, considering his level of contamination and all the other kids around and the responsibility I have, after all. Not to mention the punctilious Petra at the registration desk. Speaking of Petra, how am I supposed to get from the sauna-like solitary cell to the registration desk? Finn will probably shatter the glass walls of the cubicle in the meantime, or, if that doesn't work, bite me before I even get the chance to leave. We'll have to make it through.

Annoyed, I look for the health insurance card in my backpack. Finn screams even more eagerly. I try to focus on my breathing with all my clothes pretty much drenched in sweat while Finn is eating a cigarette butt, he found on the floor. Holding the butt, I chase to the registration desk and wait. Petra is talking with a headset on and nods at me sympathetically. She doesn't remember me, does she?

About one year prior. The crying therapy, where I was dragged under false pretenses. Finn cried a little in the first weeks, then a lot, and today not much less. But we were responsible young parents, and since osteopathy didn't do so much for our little golden boy as for the treating woman, and that was: "give as much as you can per treatment."

We decided to give up and instead – at least that's what I assumed at the time – tried to explore and optimize his sleep/wake rhythm under professional help. That was more to our liking since we wanted to sleep at night, not just in two-hour intervals. Finn had the unpleasant habit of preparing his nighttime crying by taking an extended nap in the day.

First, we received some sheets to fill out; when does he sleep, when does he cry, when does he eat. I thought it was apparent; he pretty much constantly screamed, rarely slept, and ate without interruption. Susanne thought differently.

Unfortunately, I failed to give her the sheet at 4 o'clock in the morning. We indeed would have agreed then, but the following day her night memory seemed to be entirely erased, and she didn't think the night was that bad. But how bad the nights were. I noticed these waves of activity when they were just starting to form; something was moving in the bag next to our bed, like from one corner to another with increasing speed. After a few minutes of squirming and twiddling, the vocal cords and his mother made the scene; probably flatulence, and he's too cold.

Month after month, the child was said to be too cold. I would lie next to him, sweating. One night, I moved out, and we tried to work in shifts; from 11 pm – 5 am, it was the boss's turn, after which the screaming ray of sunshine was carted to the adjoining room where I was waiting. Sitting on the bouncy ball, I would try to calm the child by stuffing him with the pacifier and emplacing Mrs. Hansen. Except for my back, this bouncing did no harm to anyone.

Once, I illegally attempted to freight the bawling creature along with his soft carrier into the bathroom – during my shift, mind you. But to no avail. One minute later, Susanne came dashing out of her room, which used to be ours, to rescue her precious darling from the unfathomable machinations of his father. It was like in the animal kingdom, right before the male lions eat their cubs. This incident has never been repeated because of the judgment I was put under by every page of professional literature and the entire pregnancy class who deemed my behavior sacrilegious and unacceptable. My failed objection of our parents had let their children scream all night was promptly shattered with, "Well, you see what came of it."

"How can I help you?" Right, I have different worries now. But whether Petra could actually help me is in doubt.

"It's about Finn. I called earlier – my goodness, about suspected chickenpox."

Thanks to the everlasting usage of 'Du', I only ever know people by their first name now, too. Petra, Petra, and what else? Even the email provider, the mobile operator, everybody greets you with "Hello Susanne Hansen." Maybe she calls herself Stankowiak or Hartmann?

Petra's hair is rigid and short, her appearance quite rigorous. Or do I just think that because of the crying therapy?

Finn was maybe 6 weeks old, and Susanne, Finn, Daddy, and a box of filled-out A4 sheets set off for the first 'session'.

Like a throne in the center of the therapy room, the treatment couch was surrounded by a few scattered chairs. There were no pictures on the walls. After briefly discussing the completed forms, the procedure began based on some particular method or school. It was not the Prague-Parent-Child-Program, but somewhat more southern, like the 'Oberpfaffenhofer School'. Babies do not cry because they are bloated, hurting, or hungry – it is all due to the sleep/wake rhythm if I remember correctly.

Finn was put on the couch, and it was now my job to get the child to sleep while the other parties were watching with wary eyes. Petra looked stern, like a driving school examiner, and Susanne was in a pretty bad mood. I can't remember why, perhaps because of those night shifts, or did the precious darling, the Schneckelchen, the Finni-Mäuschen refuse the good mother's milk? Or did I instigate another fundamental debate about "I want more fun"? I really can't remember – I don't think she liked the driving school examiner much.

First, I had to find a comfortable position on the couch next to the test person.

But there was no comfortable position as there was far too little space for me, but I didn't say anything. I was only interested in getting this episode over with as smoothly and as quickly as possible – no confrontation, only patient and benevolent nodding whenever the examiner exhibited her professional knowledge.

Finn screamed, as if somebody ordered him to, just at the right time and with all the enthusiasm we knew so well. The other participants pretended not to notice him at all, only me; I was sweating. To get this kid to sleep right here, without never-ending hobbling around on the bouncy ball, was a serious endeavor. It didn't work either. Or did he fall asleep of exhaustion after 20 minutes, maybe? Anyway, at some point, it dawned on me that it's not about the child at all. It was me who was therapized to learn baby-compatible behavior.

We didn't schedule another appointment because I couldn't say if I could take time off work next Tuesday or Thursday. We never made it back to this test. Afterward, Finn enjoyed screaming a lot and sleeping in small bits and pieces to this day. However, his boss has another opinion: it is getting better and better.

"Is he isolated," Petra asks vigorously.
"Can't you hear him?" I reply. I'm stressed out.

"'Finn Luca', there he is, but you will have to wait for at least another hour. You didn't have an appointment, did you?"

Why actually 'Finn Luca'? The child is called Finn. Don't give me those double names, like Karl-Heinz or Hans-Nico. Even during the blissful pregnancy period, when you're on the lookout for breastfeeding pillows made of probiotic spelt seed as well as first names, I vetoed them; no double names. I preferred 'Erwin' as a first name anyway. If something more modern was requested, 'Erwin Apollo' at most because I am a massive fan of the moon landing and its live reporting. Susanne thought something Nordic to be quite fancy. So, 'Erwin Apollo' was erased without replacement. The poor child! But 'Lasse' and the like were probably more fitting for the worm, which was about three cm long at the time.

To create some balance in the relationship, at least, I insisted on an alternative name. I decided on something with a more southern ring. Finally, we agreed to name the child at birth; if he was going to be blond and pale, God and others willing, it would be 'Finn'. But if his features were going to be more those of a temperamental Mafioso, he should bear the name

'Luca'. Both Susanne and Dad don't have the slightest resemblance with anything Mediterranean. We're blond and pale, like the extras in the Dr. Oetker's Rote Grütze commercials, only smaller.

Nothing you can do. One of my acquaintances had her nose chopped off and got a transplant of a resharpened version. Still, her daughter really didn't take on this plastic correction. Her hooked nose has barely any resemblance to the totally disappointed mom.

Although we were a bit hesitant when Finn was born, and a whole new name was brought up – that's another story, though – we named him Finn, and Luca as an additional name.

Most of the time, these snotty-nosed brats will be quite reproachful with the parents for the choice they made regarding their first name later on. If Finn wants to, he can switch to Luca without any significant problems. We will avoid being exposed to endless 'how could you' discussions. Not like Gönna, one of Susanne's friends, who currently has to endure accusations by her 12-year-old 'Felix': "How could you name a smart young man after smelly cat food?"

I clasp my hands together like the only dark-skinned Saint Mary of Llucmajor and pant, "At least another hour, impossible in this hovel with a child like this!"

Petra wouldn't be Petra if she didn't have a straight-off solution to this problem, "I'll bring out a surprise in a minute. It'll distract you."

Sure enough, she's been through some kind of special coaching program to calm down patients, so with my mind a bit more at ease, I go back to Finn.

When I step into the isolation tube, all my alarm bells go off, and for form's sake, every single one of my sweat glands switches to 'full output'. He is not crying!

That has never been a good sign. Not that I'm worried about Finn's health. No, the silence means something is even more interesting than noisily pushing as much air as possible through his throat. From a distance, I notice that my backpack is no longer on the stool but has been dragged to the floor where Finn is gleefully biting into some delicious treat. He would have had a choice of spelt cookies, bananas, and a piece of bunny roll.

But he picked a white candle that is about 15 cm long. My surprise is not mainly about him eating the candle, but rather why there was a candle in my backpack in the first place. I am relieved to see that neither my ID nor my bank card show any bitemarks.

Food! Dad and son are both addicted to this earthly pleasure, though with varying accentuations. One prefers heaps of meat, soap, and unrestrictedly anything that he finds on the floor. Being more of a vegetarian, the other remembers times when he prepared delicious seafood paella with lots of chili and saffron. For about 16 months, delights of that sort have been canceled due to statements like, "Leave out the spicy stuff, the peppers too, and instead of the seafood, you could cut in a little sausage!"

Well, that means canceled. Not to mention the time it all takes, everything has to be on the table immediately, not too hot and cut up into neat little bits. The times when I magically threw together a ceremonial and culinary work of art are over.

When he last visited, my older brother made the dry remark, "In this house, you get dangerously close to the table manners of the youngest member."

There are no more napkins, starters, and sitting straight at mealtimes, same as the paella. Mealtime has gradually changed too, "After all, the child needs his rhythm, and at daycare, they also eat at 11 am".

I don't feel like eating seafood at that time of day either.

Restaurant visits had to adapt to our 'new German cuisine', too. It has to be quick, there has to be a highchair available, and our precious darling needs something sausage-like, but preferably with something fancy in the title, like 'controlled farming' or something like that. Even though I know exactly that a sip from a Maggi bottle is also to his taste.

I don't even want to think about previous restaurant visits. When we last went to an Indian restaurant, it didn't go as we hoped. Finn lost his patience for his food to arrive pretty soon, even though I was in the middle of building a pipeline to the men's room to get fresh lukewarm water for his carrot juice. But it was pointless. For some reason, he didn't like that place. After lots of crying and screaming, a plate with some greens and a single tomato arrived when Finn decided to say 'thank you' by fiercely swinging his spoon. The waiter took the broken pieces to the kitchen without batting an eye.

Oh, I also remember Astrid and Saeed inviting us to the opening of their restaurant. I was really looking forward to this evening: delicious Persian food and lots of friends that I had criminally neglected over the last 16 months.

But our arrival at the 'Saray' was a bad omen already; nobody was there yet, except the waiters. In the lounge area, Finn discovered his up to this point uncharted paradise: countless candles, hookahs, ashtrays, and glasses on low little tables at a perfect clear-me-down height. Restlessly chasing after him to keep the place from burning down didn't last long. Sullen and defeated, we decided to start our retreat to eat spaghetti Aglio e Olio at home.

"Here is a book to make the time go by faster," all of a sudden, the short haircut intrudes our almost homely isolation.

Exasperated, I reply, "Are you serious? That won't last longer than two minutes. Why don't you go get the doctor, and he'll diagnose chickenpox in a wink, and we'll be on our way."

Fortunately, I didn't realize right away that the book was for six-year-olds to learn to read and therefore had only a tiny number of pictures.

"It's really not that easy!" Petra snaps.

Petra slurps back to her position while I'm still shouting some reinforcing points, such as "Thanks a lot for the help" and the like.

Finn doesn't care so much about the book; he's more interested in the other patients hurrying past us to the registration desk. I feel like I've seen this all before – I know it all, but in reversed roles and not at the pediatrician, but at the zoo. All the parents naturally keep their sensitive sprouts away from us outcasts. If I had something to write on with me, I would hang a sign in our cubicle saying: "Keep away from the cage" or "… no feeding allowed".

One of my main problems in watching Finn is that I suffer from boredom and the feeling of being out of my depth at the same time.

That's how it goes: I'm sitting there while Finn is trying to stack two matchboxes on top of each other, and he's trying and trying. I might say "well" before my ciliary muscle relaxes and my mind wanders. Not even a second later, I'm trying to save the child from suffocating because some matches got stuck crosswise in his throat.

Same here in the isolation chamber. Out of nowhere, the doctor's assistant is standing in front of me and unexpectedly rips me out of my own thoughts – what a shame. My mind had beautifully slipped away, and I was paddling on a big lake in a solo canoe; it was so lovely and peaceful and lonely. "Well, that's certainly not what the inventor had in mind! Please take him in quickly before the doctor is here in a moment," says the helper. This one I also remember from our last visit. We were in the helicopter room. Finn wasn't interested in the toys and the helicopter car that had been set up at all. Instead, he liked the desk with all the chrome instruments and the patient files and the computer keyboard much more.

Without warning, this assistant stood behind us, trying to type Finn's medical history into the computer. "What's going on here. Nothing's in place, and the mouse... Where's the mouse?"

Finn said, "Daaah!" and pointed up to the ceiling. I said nothing and looked down to the floor.

"No, Finn, what are you doing?" I call out, annoyed. Outside the cabin, Finn is trying to maneuver the only wilted flowerpot down to the ground. He probably wants a clear view of Karstadt, or to be more exact, the beloved animal department on the first floor of Karstadt, or maybe even the slide in the children's play area on the 4th floor.

I jump to my feet and drag him back into the box, where there's no more room for turning and bending at this point. For my taste, I'm standing way too close to the doctor's assistant, not to mention the unbearable heat and – of course – Finn. Finn is grinning at her as if he's overcome with joy. I wonder if he suspects that things are getting more interesting for him now. I throw him onto the worn plastic cover and frantically undress him. The assistant is incessantly asking questions again, which I reply to without much focus. It's simply not possible for me to undress or dress the kicking child while performing any other activity at the same time. If this was part of my skill set, I would have certainly started training as a flight captain at Airbus. The assistant doesn't seem to care – and neither do I, so I reply without sense or reason.

Now, the doctor also enters the single square meter and compassionately pats me on the shoulder: "There's our Blondy."

Blondy looks up and begins to mobilize oxygen from the deepest depths of his lungs to unleash an excessively intense roar. The pediatrician, Dr. Schmitterts, calms me down and says, "A classic case of fear of strangers." I remember our last doctor's visit, knocking, Blondy being scared of strangers; it was just like today; the only difference was that it happened in the helicopter room, and I talked to the doctor then. Today I speak to Dr. Schmitterts' chest that is 10 cm away from my face.

"He has chickenpox, and we need a note for the daycare."

The chest replies, "Let's take a look inside his mouth. The conditions couldn't be any better right now." Finn is shrieking as if someone is about to chop off his limbs, even though none of the people present – neither the doctor nor the nurse – is touching him.

"Well, that looks good!" the chest enunciates. Even though I'm standing on my backpack now for lack of space, Mr. Schmitterts seems to be a particularly long specimen. Looking up, I notice that the space between the ceiling and the doctor's hairdo is not bigger than the width of my hand. Then he catches me staring and apologizes.

"It's too bad the halogen spotlights went belly-up again. We constantly have to replace them." I'm in doubt if the spots weren't turned off on purpose to protect Mr. Schmitt's hairstyle from any damages in the isolation chamber, but instead, I yell, "The good old light bulbs... those were the days."

Susanne believes that Finn's animosity towards the doctor is due to his habit of dressing exclusively in black and his gray hair. I'm not so sure about that. My older brother is also gray-haired and prefers the architect's uniform. Finn, however, always finds him pretty adorable. The good thing about the thunderous screaming is that it shortens the examination time by quite a bit.

After about two minutes, the chest is strongly inclined to leave the contaminated site stating, "Chickenpox, clearly chickenpox!". However, I try to stop him, "I observed something else there."

Reluctantly he decelerates but immediately gains control – now outside the box: "What's the matter?"

I'm not sure what to say before I reply: "Recently, we noticed that Finn has been foaming at the mouth more and more often. I mean, air bubbles are coming out of his mouth. Do you think this has anything to do with the rash, perhaps?"

No, I didn't say "rabies" and actually wasn't planning on asking anything like that at all. But Susanne told me to ask the doctor about the bubbles and Finn's constantly sweaty feet, and I forgot the third thing.

"Aha, Blondy is a little bubble machine," I hear the doctor's mocking tone, "Let's put him in the middle of the waiting room, so all the other kids will get something out of it, too." Everyone laughs. I'm somewhat embarrassed by my stupid question. On the other hand, he is somewhat triumphant because of his brilliant joke, and the assistant is somewhat constrained because of her employment.

Then he's gone, and the assistant is talking to me alone: "Please wait here for just a moment. I'll get you a prescription." She disappears, and so does Finn's sobbing. I get off my backpack.

Finn is always quite affectionate after his bouts of crying, and Dad savors this brief time with him. He babbles, "NEE-NA-NA," I reply, "Aha, alright."

"NEE-NA-NA," I respond, "Yes yes, little Finn." After repeating the conversation for the umpteenth time, I can hear the passing fire truck and reply,

"Nee-Naw-Nee-Naw!" His face breaks into a wide grin, and he replies firmly, "NEE-NA-NA," and we are both happy. The black and gray monster is gone, the disease definitely confirmed, and we can start our way home soon.

After packing up the candle, the remaining food, and the child, we leave our acquainted glass box in different directions. Finn wants to take the door to the registration desk, and I walk towards the exit. "Well, where does our silly little boy want to go?" says Dad derisively and drags him to the correct door. Why would he want to get any closer to his screaming epicenter again?

As soon as we arrive in the stairwell, I can hear Petra yelling after us: "And what about the prescription?"

"Oh yeah," I reply, trying to grab the prescription. "Apply to the blisters three times a day and be careful not to get it in his eyes, or there will be lots of screaming," she instructs me.

"Right then, screaming, you say!" I reply more absently than obediently listening, finally snatching the piece of paper from her.

Chapter 2

Once downstairs, reasonably safe and sound, we set off in the direction of Mozart Pharmacy. I'm pushing the stroller with my right hand, and with my left, I'm navigating my bike. At the same time, I'm trying to catch and throw back all the objects Finn hurls out of his stroller.

This game I know too well: with his foot, he hoists his bottle overboard while his tiny right hand chucks his hat onto the sidewalk, only to take advantage of me diving down to grab the items and to dump the remaining stuff on the other side of the stroller.

Entering the Mozart Pharmacy on Wiener Straße, I ask myself: When was the last time I went to a pharmacy for my own issues?

Dagmar made me aware of this the other day via email.

Dagmar, a former classmate, is sitting somewhere at Lake Constance, and no matter when and how often I write her a mail – she replies straight away. How much time does she have to sit at the computer?

The landscape around Lake Constance is quite distinctive. Here in the recreation area around Berlin, things look a bit different. I'm not necessarily infatuated with the Märkische wasteland, though I know my way around. I skimmed almost every dirt track with my bike to publish a hinterland bike map outside the market. Infertile soil and pines as far as the eye can see at best interrupted by the brownish broth of a lake.

Right, Dagmar, who also enjoys participating in afternoon TV talk shows discussing topics, such as 'My husband, the prick.' I think she understands these TV appearances as PR opportunities to hold her new but poorly received novel, including the web address, into the camera.

Dagmar asked me recently where my hypochondria had gone.

"No frightening diseases ever since Finn was born? What's the matter? Did you run out of breath?"

She's right. But what does she mean by 'not being sick' anymore? I've been permanently sick for the past 16 months. Finn shoots everything at me, like the sniffles which I've had for five weeks now. No one has the sniffles for that long, only me and the mobs.

But Dagmar is right. For two years, I have had no raging heart attacks, suspected colon cancer, or even self-diagnosed brain tumors. Indeed. But how am I supposed to get time to go to the doctor with things like that? The days when I consolidated specialist after specialist because of suspected heart attacks are gone. I can still remember Prof. Bebler, a cardiologist who, after vehemently insisting on my part, examined and scanned me for half a day. Terrible heart muscle spasms left me fearfully sweating and vegetating for weeks. His verdict: Every single one of his patients who are currently sitting in his waiting room would gleefully swap their heart for mine. Harsh words, but the stinging was gone; no, it actually moved up to the eye the next day... Or my aching ankle. The ortho-pedist, who was an insider tip from Susanne's preg-nancy yoga teacher, quickly concluded, "Obviously, the pain stems from a low kidney position."

Finally, there was someone who recognized my pain and was willing to find its cause. Afterward, I had to go to countless osteopath appointments – each time, I had to pay 30 Euros. And I had to put up a lot of effort during the treatments. As I was lying on the treatment bench, with him on top of me pressing into my stomach, we tried to push my right kidney back towards the liver, threatening it with brute force. After ten treatments, I asked the gruff artist if the kidney wouldn't fall back down if I stood up. Hesitantly he replied, "Well." I think this "well" and the constant grind were responsible for my ankle not feeling like hurting anymore, not to mention the abdominal pain from being pulled up.

Finn doesn't like the pharmacy. A curly head appears behind the counter who I dutifully hand the prescription. The curly head is the owner of this pharmacy. I know him.

After canceling the crying therapy, Kerstin, our – or rather Susanne's – midwife, had another brilliant idea: "Maybe your little sunshine can't fill his tummy at mommy's breast, and he cries because he's hungry."

A new guess always calls for a new therapeutic approach. This time we were supposed to weigh the child before and after sucking. Then there were more tables about age and grams per breastfeeding and day and week and so on. But of course, we had to use a special scale from the pharmacy, which I borrowed from the curly head at that time. No, not one but three different ones. We always believed that the scales were not in good order. The measurement result was often lower after breastfeeding than before, which could only be due to the scale.

After a few weeks, Finn and I returned the last borrowed scale to the Mozart Pharmacy. Finn was screaming at the top of his lungs when we arrived, so we didn't have to wait until it was our turn. The curly head took the scales and said: "Ohh, that probably was for nowt."

Today, I believe that Finn's weight loss was more likely related to the sometimes liquid, sometimes solid substances he secreted, rather than a lack of sucking. The midwife rarely recognized simple explanations of that sort: "He's not there yet. I can tell by his typical circular movements. Give the little worm some more time." You couldn't beat her in her timing. After about 58 minutes, she got up and went to the door, "And if anything comes up, call me. I'm not on duty next weekend, though." How did she always know when the 60 minutes were up? Every weekend we had to call her substitute for advice because we were at our wits' end – week after week and weekend after weekend.

The midwife had no children herself, but as she always stressed that she owned a cat. At that time, I could imagine why: she prefers purring to screaming. In my opinion, she didn't have Finn under control. At some point, she put it in a nutshell: "You've got quite a strong-willed son there. You'll have to toughen up, or he'll be walking all over you." Toughen up in the sense of being disciplined and consistent. If that's what she meant, we still haven't been able to put it into practice.

The owner hands me a package of anti-itch cream and another medicine over the counter. Quite swiftly, we leave the scale pharmacy.

Unfortunately, I don't pay attention to the imperative safety distance between Finn's wingspan and the not firmly cemented world. The snotty brat somehow manages to stretch out to a donation box on a shelf that noisily clatters on the stone floor. Annoyed, I look up to the ceiling. Finn follows my example, and Dad picks up the box off the floor: donations for the Protestant Tabor congregation.

Wasn't that the association that sent me a card for my 40th birthday and even called me to wish me a happy birthday? Never heard from them before.

From 40 onwards, the church believes that it's time for you to think about God and death and the Tabor congregation. The grim reaper is already waving at you at the horizon. And no one should be able to complain that nobody warned them in time.

A little later, I took revenge on this association for their marketing campaign by rejecting their request for a solar plant when I was working as a committee member for the allocation of public funds. To this day, I'm still the victim of evil looks here and there whenever I meet the church official. If he only knew that our son was sitting in his very own kindergarten.

Chapter 3

Susanne was quite paranoid: we need to baptize the child. I didn't really care, and if I did, I would have preferred Buddhism.

But our boss insisted on proper Christianity and had the privilege of determining the time, place, and procedure. Just below Denmark, right at the North Sea, where she herself was baptized, everything was supposed to take place. My parents and my older brother took a flight to Hamburg and continued in a rental car. My sister, her husband, and their children Annika and Katharina endued ten excruciating hours in their car on the highway across the republic. Ingrid, the one who's hanging on to my big brother, arrived one day later and left one day early. I think she likes family gatherings as much as I do.

We crammed the entire crew into a converted windmill near the Witzworter church.

Susanne's family – parents and brother with Natalie and three children – lived in that nest anyway. We didn't want to invite any more guests.

We were supposed to present the baptismal chant and some song suggestions at a baptismal meeting prior to the actual baptism. Unfortunately, I couldn't attend this ecclesiastical event and gave Susanne a few suggestions from my extensive online search for "baptismal chants." Piety was somewhat secondary in my suggestions, but I forgot the actual chant that Susanne and the pastor picked – probably something about helping others and doing good.

I still remembered the pastor from Grandma Hansen's funeral: pious looking, much younger than Susanne and me, always trying to hide his far too many teeth by pressing his lips together. This lip-squeezing looked like a permanent grin. But he actually was quite friendly.

He had produced an incredible number of children and still didn't look as tired as we did.

The night before the "festivities", the mill became the scene of some jolly tippling while I had to support Klärchen, Susanne's mother, and her nervousness starting from 10 pm. Somehow, she got behind schedule once again. Because of her overly focused approach, she had some problems with the two frozen dough balls in front of her. "I can't even remember if I put baking soda in the dough. What am I supposed to do now?" moaned Klärchen.

"No problem, we'll just put it in a bit later," I tried to calm her down, thinking that I had nothing better to do.

I stood in Klärchen's kitchen and tossed one packet of baking soda after another into the dough, which had at least partially thawed in the microwave. While I was kneading, Susanne was busy with herself, Johann with his sleep, and Klärchen with her many questions.

"Don't you think the dough tastes too much like baking soda now?" asked Klärchen.

"Absolutely not!" was my confident reply, as if I were a born baking soda specialist. Baking isn't really my thing. With all the stirring and scrambling and burnt results. Quite the opposite of cooking and the breezy bubbling along. Of course, I heavily doubted if my brutal tossing of baking soda was the right thing to do: Can you actually taste baking soda, or by how much does a dough double in size with too much leavening?

"Couldn't you finish the whole cake?" continued, or rather asked, Susanne's mother.

"Not really! I don't even know what you want to bake, and I also really need to..." I can't remember my excuse anymore, but I had no desire whatsoever to form this dumpling, top it, decorate it, and put it in and out of the oven.

Already I could feel another question mark arise behind my back: "I'm really not sure now. Did I put baking soda in the dough before freezing it, after all? At least in one of them. But in which one? And now, there's way too much baking soda in there. What are we going to do?"

The questions were getting fuzzier and fuzzier as I got closer to my bed. Even in the middle of the night, countless question marks were shot at me, and I could only think: What is she doing? or better, What is she asking and above all whom?

The Lord's Day began more amusingly than I suspected. Before the baptism, the entire crew wanted to attend the regular church service under the theme of "Bible Sunday." The mill arrived in a small motorcade. Johann and Klärchen and Susanne's brother Klaus ran to the church on foot. We stayed with the child since our little golden boy and his parents still had some grooming to do.

At the window, I saw how the entire mill, including Susanne's parents, was rushing back to said mill after less than ten minutes. What was going on?

Unfortunately, except for our crew and the sacristan, not a single soul had shown up. That is nothing new for the faithless north.

But the pastor should already be there! Susanne's brother, Klaus, quickly became aware of the situation: "Last night they played village ball, and they've probably poured a little too much in the pastor's glass."

He went to the pastor's house to wake him up, and all the required people appeared for the baptism in time, which took place after the service. The mill had killed time once again with the help of alcoholic beverages, and the pastor didn't look particularly good.

Besides Finn, there was another baptism. The local pimp's grandchild. The pimp himself was not present. I can't remember if Susanne said he was in jail or killed himself.

I got the impression that the pastor didn't take the entire event very seriously. First and foremost, his voice was hardly perceptible, later he mixed up the children's names to be baptized, and the songs that Susanne had carefully selected were canceled. The event was over in no time.

The meal in the Rote Haubarg, on the other hand, lasted way too long. Finn felt the urge to constantly clean up the table while Klärchen did the same to her stomach afterward.

To my big surprise, Johann had a lot of fun with Ingrid. He is usually pretty stubborn and uncommunicative, quite introverted, or asleep.

My father, "Schorschi", bent everybody's ear with his Latin verses for the remaining time of the feast.

No, not all of them. Klärchen, who once had to study Latin at school, was excited about his knowledge. My father, on the other hand, never studied it at school. And we all knew his phrases, like "o tempera, o mores." It wasn't until Christmas that I had to take him to the emergency room because of his bowel obstruction. Between his screaming fits, chunks of Latin were flying at the hopelessly overwhelmed medical assistant. His Latin skills were even poorer than his medical ones: "'O tempera, o mores,' I do not know. Where in the world is my colleague?"

In the afternoon, the mill served cream cakes for the Northerners and cheesecake with red wine for the inhabitants from the far South. Klärchen's night shift cake was now called applesauce cake and fortunately didn't exceed the tolerated standard height for baked goods. Perhaps only just because Klärchen had scalped away the burnt lower third.

I thought the cake tasted quite good compared to the multitude of cream cakes. It didn't matter whether they were called Black Forest Cake or something else. They all tasted like cream and butter. They only varied in decoration, either a cherry, a nut, or other name-giving accessories.

Conclusion: a lampshade burned out in the mill, I got herpes all over my thigh, and Susanne's entire set of silverware has since disappeared, and her black blazer is also gone. Instead, we now own an extra towel with the inscription "sauna", and we should have a baptism candle somewhere in the apartment.

Finn hasn't shown any signs of a Christian attitude whatsoever until today. But he is not really an exception. Most children on the playground are incredibly mean and nasty with each other. At times, there's even deliberate spitting and biting. Only the mothers surpass this behavior. Woe is Finn if he borrows a small form from another child. Not only does the victim tear and tug at his property: the mom comes over knowing no barriers to the manners of coexistence.

It must be the protective instinct. It seems that this has already been domesticated to an alarming degree, since it is not so much the child protected as these little sand molds. According to my knowledge, fathers are different, somehow less involved, and busy with other things. They read the newspaper, or gamble, or daydream instead of protecting their brood. But only so long until the mother species interrupts and enters the fight for their most sacred possession. How many times I've thought, "Make it rain red molds!" But I keep my mouth shut.

Susanne has fewer problems with the molds, but she knows the issue of mothers and their beastliness very well. My big brother calls this phenomenon "cattiness" when you can hear exchanges between mothers, like "Oh poor you, the hardest time with the little one is ahead of you. I'm just happy we got through it!", or "You're not that chubby anymore now that you've weaned."

I am spared such caresses. But I notice that other moms tend to turn their heads after me on the street. No, not quite after me, but after the stroller fixing their gaze on the child while tilting their head slightly. But woe is me if I catch them at it.

Now we are finally leaving the Mozart Pharmacy, and I am thinking about how we will best spend our time until 8 pm. We could kill at least another hour at the children's farm in Görlitzer Park, or we could visit Mom at her practice. The Mom-option is riskier. The waiting room could be full, and Finn would be able to his beloved Mom for maybe 18 seconds. And I wouldn't have gained much time other than those 18 seconds, but probably a giant temper tantrum when leaving the practice.

One time, we were ordered to wait and hold there. Finn had immediately dragged some plaster dentures from a shelf while I was trying to match the name-plates to the plaster casts. I hopefully succeeded considering the vast amount of lower jaw dentures. Mom could hear her Finni-baby screaming while she was treating a patient and couldn't focus very well. We secretly left when a box with some other spare parts fell over. Susanne was a bit upset. Letting go is not exactly her biggest strength.

I remember Mom's first time letting go. Dad gave the two-month-old new Mom theater tickets and planned to keep the flag flying at home. Susanne was a little late, and her friend Carla was waiting outside the theater.

Unfortunately, breastfeeding under such conditions is quite fruitless, although Finn was roaring at the top of his lungs at both breasts. I'm sure the breasts were mentally already at the theater. The child fell asleep, only to start screaming again right after Mom left.

My possibilities were relatively limited after all. It was the good mother's milk that was demanded, and for the last hour of waiting, we both screamed.

Somehow the time until the theater visitor returned passed, and the child knocked around the breasts, and the Mommy sobbed: "I will never leave my golden little darling again."

Mom's second attempt took some time. She didn't want to miss the annual three-girlfriend-get-together.

Merle from Zurich, Conny from Hamburg, and Susanne planned to meet somewhere beyond the dike for a long weekend.

Finn had to throw up a lot and intensely the night before departure before also developing a fever and other symptoms. With a heavy heart, Mom took off towards the dike, and Dad joined his poor little guy a day later with a particularly severe form of gastro-enteritis.

Carrying Finn, I tottered from bush to bush to empty my insides. Our beloved golden boy started laughing at the top of his lungs each and every time I disappeared in the bushes, which made me even more desperate. Did he think I was something like a swing with a built-in fountain? I could have died – he thought it was hilarious.

Anyway, Susanne came back in a crabby mood Sunday evening to find us exhausted and sniveling on the kitchen floor. Mom got infected on the dot, so all three of us could pass the bowl at night. Susanne could finally spend more time with her darling – and I'm talking about Finn.

I pick the children's farm for timing reasons.

I don't have the best relationship with animals. I used to own a tomcat called "Veit von Stichelstein."

But I was already 17, and it didn't last very long as he was dismantled by a car quite soon after I got him.

Yes, I kind of like insects with their compound eyes, but the larger the animal, the more threatening it seems to me.

With Finn, things look a bit different. He reaches out his little hand with the old bunny roll offering it to the donkeys. And as soon as they want to grab it, he snaps it away and pleasurably gobbles it up or decides to share it cordially once more. He plays this game with the goats, sheep, geese, and rabbits too.

Afterward, we squat in the sandbox for a short while and argue about the ownership of the bucket and shovel until it's time to go.

We meet Fine and her mother at the pigsty, where 'Pippi, the stinky, fat pot-bellied pig' lives. Fine is one of Finn's fellow students, meaning a fellow kindergartener. Her mother tells me that they had chickenpox (by "we," she means, of course, the child had the pox and the parents had the trouble) and had gone on vacation to Gomera for two weeks.

"And what was it like there?" I ask enviously and not worried anymore since Finn's pox can probably no longer find a breeding ground with Fine.

"Well, it's just different to what it used to be. In the first week, Fine had stomach problems so that we couldn't go on hikes as much, and the little ones just sleep better back home."

I'm familiar with this expression: "different." It sounds like some things have changed, but in my opinion, it is a synonym for "not as good as before."

"What do you actually do for a living?" the mother asks me distractedly.

"What do you do in the city of underemployed web designers?" I snappily reply while vigorously tugging at Finn's hat.

"Oh, you're a designer. That's interesting. You certainly work at night when Finn Luca is asleep?"

I don't reply but yell, "No, Finn, that's not yours!" One of the enormous advantages of being somewhere with your child! Pulling off a red herring is always an option and usually successful. In the blink of an eye, I'm running after him.

Fine's mother also has other things to do, as Fine has just found an appetite for goat food. While Fine's mother is trying to fish the stuff out of her daughter's maw, she yells at us: "We'll see you tomorrow at the daycare."

Chapter 4

The daycare, or German "Kita". I prefer "kindergarten". A place to thrive and blossom. In Finn's group, there are four boys and six girls, plus Heike and Christine. Altogether, they're called the "Teddys". There is another group with a different name but similar children and concepts.

Since Susanne wanted or had to go back to work at the beginning of the year, I was assigned the serious task of getting the child through the acclimatization process.

The very first contact with the kindergarten teachers was, in my eyes, a waste of time. I took the subject to the educational treatment room in time at 9:30 a.m. When we arrived, five children were running rampantly in a quadrangle. The two pedagogues put me into place straight away by harassing me and luring me into deceitful traps: "For heaven's sake, everybody who still has shoes on, take them off immediately."

Who could they possibly mean?

"Next time, all 'unaccustomed' parents, please show up on time," the attempts at intimidation continued.

Finn was gone, yanking a telephone dummy that another child was tugging on the other side. I sat down on the floor – now shoeless – and a girl brought me more toys than I honestly cared for that morning. This particular child had quite an unpleasant smell, and I didn't know if I was authorized to suggest a diaper change.

I said, "How does this work now?"

No answer. The two important people had utterly different worries: They talked about some train connection and the audacity of the railroad officials to have somehow set the schedule wrong. Then they continued their chat with highly political Berlin problems and their solution dropping keywords like 'debt reduction' and 'restructuring'.

By now, Finn wanted to leave again. So did I. I repeated my question, "How does this work now?"

The smelly girl was pressing herself against my back. Then there was a response: "Well, would you prefer the rough method or the gentle one, the one that's more pleasant for the child?" asked Christine.

Actually, I wanted to know who looked after all those children here and who would change the girl's diaper. But I said, "What do you mean with 'rough'? Finn has been coming here with Susanne for four weeks. That's not rough."

"Well, you'll know what you can square with your conscience. Unfortunately, we can't ask Finn Luca?" Both of them grinned at me.

I chose the rough way and was allowed to leave for 20 minutes afterward. What do you do in January on Cuvrystraße outside of the daycare for 20 minutes? Drown in boredom! And wait and very slowly go back inside and pick up Finn.

This little game went on for a week. Then the two top dogs detected a fever of 38.2 degrees and a cold and pronounced a Kita ban – no ifs and or buts. It all dragged on much longer and more namby-pamby than I had suspected. But from February onwards, Finn had finally settled.

But now we'll go home. No, the child needs food supplies since everything edible has been fed. We make a brief pitstop at the bakery on Cuvrystraße just below our old apartment. The stroller and the bicycle have to wait outside.

As usually, "the scraggy one" serves us. We dutifully wait in line, and Finn turns to me with a "mama". I don't react. However, the grandma behind me does, "Hello, your daughter is calling you. Don't you hear her?" I nod in confusion. Certainly, Finn's red jacket, but I'm not aware of anything feminine on me.

"A bunny roll as always?" asks the scraggy one.

Nodding, I put Finn down. Outside, I can see a mutt trying to pee on my bike. I sprint through the door to threaten it with a fake kick. From outside, I can see Finn smearing his squishy bunny roll on the glass case while dripping carrot juice on the terracotta tiles with the other hand. I rush up to him, "No, Finn, not the eggs."

I manage to save the pack of eggs. I'm not so sure about the terracotta tiles. Kneeling on the floor, cleaning the glass case, and holding Finn, a corpulent maybe 30-year-old customer, speaks down to me: "One thing I can tell you. It doesn't get any better!" and points to her two somewhat older children.

My older brother would call that a successful catty remark. Or as he likes to say, "Hello, I'm mommy with a full tummy." I'm just afraid she's right.

Speaking of 'older brother'. He wanted to give me a very special gift for my last birthday: "I'm inviting you to cross the Alps with me by bike."

Typical childless big brothers, I thought. Where should I get the stamina from? Yes, in the past, I used to go running three times a week, took my bike out a lot, and felt like I was in good shape. But today, everything is totally different. I've got hardly any time to exercise – except for pushing the stroller.

He didn't even worry about who would look after Finn. Did he expect Susanne to take some days off so that she could pick him up from the daycare on Tuesday and Thursday at 2:30 p.m.? Oh, the big brothers. I politely turned the offer down.

We quickly leave the spot on the terracotta tile before the scraggy one gets the chance to claim recourse.

There used to be a traditional bakery here without particularly biologically sound flours and much cheaper: the Siontek bakery.

Unfortunately, it seemed as if the team had little motivation. Usually, around early afternoon, all relatively edible baked goods were sold out. Shelf-stable and preserved pretzels, marshmallow mice, and chewing gum were still available.

I remember one beautiful afternoon. The shop assistant, a Kreuzberger woman about to retire, was faced with a long customer line. Unfortunately, the display was nothing but a yawning void. Everyone in the line was craving a sweet temptation. One particularly brave customer bleated from behind my back: "Don't you have any more goods, not even a Plunderstück or Bienenstich, nothing at all?"

The shop assistant replied: "Naught, Sir."

He didn't let up. "Then please take a look back in the bakery. This isn't possible."

She actually went. The line waited patiently, hoping for a full tray of delicious baked goods. And waited. It took forever for our bakery lady to reappear from behind the curtain to the bakery in the back: "All finished!!!" she mumbled while devouring the last bite of something that was no longer identifiable.

Now she was standing in front of us with her mouth dusted with icing sugar, and the brave customer behind me went off, "You ate the last bit and didn't leave anything for us, you silly cow!"

No one took a marshmallow mouse, though the bakery lady touted them like chopped liver while wiping her mouth. A few months later, that bakery chain went out of business, and our bakery lady got her well-deserved retirement.

Outside the bakery, we meet our neighbor from our old apartment: "There's my sunshine," Olivia says happily.

When Finn was born, she gave him a teddy bear. Since we named all stuffed toys after their givers, this one is called "Olivia Newton-John". It seems to be a popular model, as we also got a "Natalie" and a "Hilke" that only differ in size. Well, that's not true; "Hilke" is a sheep. "Janka", a wobbly polar bear, is my favorite. Finn likes "Dr. Sveni", but of course, by far the undisputed favorite is "Mrs. Hansen".

Mom sweated on a cloth diaper when she was pregnant so that the little sweetheart would never have to miss her scent. After knotting up some string at the top and tying a thread a little lower, this cloth received the name "Mrs. Hansen".

Now, this diaper looks like a deformed, tumor-infested voodoo doll, only much spookier. But what's really convenient about it is how easy it is to duplicate it. Sweat, string, thread, and it's done. "Mrs. Hansen" currently exists in three versions: one is at home, one is in the daycare, and one is in the washing machine.

Finni-baby is happy to see the ex-neighbor, also because of the big black mutt next to her and the burning cigarette butt in the corner of her mouth.

I recognize the puppy as the pissing prick from before and am somewhat relieved that I didn't really kick it because of the good neighborly relations.

"Well, how are you and Riccardo?" I ask while keeping a close eye on the mutt, named "Saskia."

What an inappropriate name. This specimen is an immensely huge, pitch-black, and very danger-ous-looking fighting dog. However, Susanne says: "Nonsense. This dog is in no way huge and definitely no 'fighting dog'", but I can literally smell his aggres-siveness. It would undoubtedly have ripped apart my front wheel if I had not courageously scared it off.

"Riccardo" is her husband. Half our age and orig-inally from a hicksville near Klein Trebbow near Schwerin. Olivia grew up "outside," as her 1st-floor grandma used to say. That means somewhere on the outskirts in Lichtenrade, or Mariendorf, or Lankwitz or something.

She was always quite fond of Finn, as she also desperately wanted to have children. Unfortunately, despite psychological as well as medical help, it didn't work out for her. Riccardo was to blame, or more precisely his sperm, or to be exact, the lack of Riccardo's sperm, so they turned to breed snakes, fish, cormorants, and looking after this mutt. I had always refused to fill in when it came to feeding these critters.

"Mustn't grumble, eh?" Olivia replies, breathing a big cloud of smoke towards us. "Unemployed – both – now! They caught Riccardo when something was missing in the cash register. But they got something coming. Friday, we're going to the lawyer."

The mutt is eating Finn's bunny roll, and wondering if dogs can also get chickenpox, I say, "Oh, that's too bad."

"What about your new apartment?"

Oh yes, we had to move. Actually, the apartment was quite nice. I would have liked a balcony, but thanks to our offspring, space was becoming increasingly scarce.

When she was pregnant, Susanne dragged home anything that money could buy and somehow fit through our apartment door. No, not just new items, like a huge nursing pillow that was never used.

When she was out to buy a child's car seat, Susanne came back with a rocking horse, which the seller of the seat apparently threw in for free. It was and still is also the packaging that is dragged into the apartment. "I could cover the box with pretty posters for Finn to have a cozy tiny house to play in. I used to love that as a child."

To this day, Susanne still buys new items daily, and I'm afraid we'll be moving again soon. Maybe to the substation next door.

My passion for shopping, on the other hand, has declined tremendously. I remember a T-shirt that I bought for Finn. It was green and "Police" was printed on it. Another example of a counterpoint to textiles with inscriptions like "My sweet baby". The little rascal wore this shirt only once on Rügen. Many passers-by greeted me reverently until I realized: They think this has to be the son of a proud policeman who would like his heir to follow in his professional footsteps. Ever since that holiday on Rügen, I have never bought any other pieces of clothing for him.

Rügen. That was a wonderful vacation.

My older brother and Ingrid – the one who transmuted Johann's temper at the baptism – had invited us there for a couple of days. Ingrid didn't do so much transmuting back then, and at three in the morning, Susanne's was already up and out in front of the cabin to rock the squaller around the square.

During the day, I got a turquoise-colored bag, which was tied at the back with a big bow. That way, I was supposed to take our little dumpling on a hike. Susanne had borrowed this hideous sack from Astrid, the friend with the Persian restaurant. I looked like a kangaroo that was unfortunately dyed turquoise and missed the mark in the chase race.

Why my older brother and Ingrid always have to run on outings of that sort, I don't want to know. In any case, it was always awfully hard for me to keep pace while hopping after them.

But eventually, I didn't have to wear the turquoise-colored apron anymore. The kangaroo and Finn were to go on an excursion by themselves. Ingrid and the older brother were leaving earlier and earlier, and Susanne was fed up to the back teeth because of her night shifts.

As we were hopping towards the forest, Finn fell asleep quickly. So, I decided to enjoy a comfortable snooze myself, and a few hours later, we walked the 300 meters back to the cabin.

Since Mom believed that the sack was pinching Finn's legs and they looked pretty blue, that was the last day of the kangaroo. I think that the dye that Astrid applied to the cloth was coming off, but it was just fine with me. We left a few days early and a little tired.

"Yes, the new apartment is nice. It's just a shame that the kindergarten is right where the old apartment was. Now we have to cart the child 20 minutes back and forth every day," I reply to Olivia.

I kept quiet about the new balcony and the different ways to use it. Susanne suggested to either put up some rabbit hutches or redesign the whole area into a sandbox. I see things a bit differently. I would prefer some chairs, a lounger, some green stuff, and a small grill.

Chapter 5

To be honest, I've been a little worried about the change in Susanne's taste. We used to furnish our apartment in a very humble way, with more space to live and less clutter.

Today, everything important and fragile hangs one meter above the ground, regardless of whether this contributes to a sense of space or not. There's useless stuff all around, which apparently "doesn't look so bad" after all.

For example, the bathroom: umpteen plugs to hang toothbrushes. One looks like a dinosaur, one like a frog, one like a little bear, and yet we have a plain glass as a toothbrush container. They all drop to the floor together with the brushes from time to time.

Well, actually only Finn's brushes. Ours don't fit in the plug holder; they are too thick. By now, Susanne has matched the number of Finn's toothbrushes to the number of plugs. Next to them is a washcloth that looks like a turtle. On the towel is a Christmas embroidery. Next to it is a little bear costume to wrap our little Finni baby in after he had his bath. Beneath sits a battery of squeaky yellow ducks, but each in a different design and size.

Opposite the bathroom is quite an impressive double door that is 2.8 meters tall and leads into the study. For the past two weeks, this door has been deprived of its actual purpose, namely, to allow people to pass through it. Instead, we stretched a swing from one side of the doorframe to the other, but Finn squats inside the swing only once in a while.

Now, I have to walk across the hallway and the dining room and step over the big pasted-up box and the new tricycle to enter the study.

But that will change soon anyway. Why do we even need a study, especially one that is so big? Sooner or later, this will become Finn's kingdom because the poor little jellybean will never be able to really thrive in his small room.

Besides the beautiful balcony, the chamber, which was supposed to eventually become Finn's, was elementary for me to choose this apartment. I thought, since Finn's room is located in the back, we would have our peace in the evening and at night in the other rooms facing the street. What a fallacy.

This case of swapping rooms seems to have been creeping on for a while. In addition to the mentioned tricycle, I can see this giant box that Mom has plastered with photos in the middle of the room. On top, as some kind of roof, she put up an umbrella. But it's no ordinary one: it's red with black dots and two antennae.

Inside the box are a few teddy bears, such as "Grandma Hop". Even the inside of the giant box is covered with posters of adorable bunnies. Next to the giant box is another box about the size of the isolation cubicle at the pediatrician's office; only much lower; and without a suction device. Inside there are dozens of plastic animals, a plastic forest, and plastic rock landscapes. And it all looks as if a devastating earthquake happened just a minute ago.

A couple of clothespins and my sunglasses, as well as the income tax return from 2002, somehow remind you of the study it used to be, even though somebody decoratively incorporated them into the landscape inferno.

Between the plastered giant box and the inferno, there is an inflatable armchair with floral applications, which to this day I have not yet perceived as an existing inventory of the apartment.

A cuddly blanket is wrapped around the entire ensemble. The imprints are probably very educationally valuable: airplane, bus with children and cats, car with child behind the wheel and mutt on the passenger seat, and tractor with mutated giant mice on the trailer.

Underneath this locomotion theme park blanket is a small storybook with an awfully drawn signet. It's not surprising that the publisher decided to print a description underneath each picture just to be sure: 'cat', 'milk', 'cake'.

Finn will never recognize this illustration as a cake: a square flat yellow box with eight holes and a dividing line.

The text the publisher put on the cover reads: "You can look through this little cardboard book with your child. The simple illustrations will help them to playfully learn new words."

I'm really not a pedagogue, but I'm sure that new words with this type of new connotation certainly throw the little rascals off their actual path of learning.

I won't get into describing the dining room since this is actually the room where the three of us spend most of our time. That's why most toys are scattered around here too. However, Finn doesn't seem to care much about this stuff.

His favorite things are telephones, laptops, televisions, and drills that work the way they're supposed to. Now and then, a washing machine, a dishwasher, a refrigerator to open and close, and Finn's world is fine. It's just that the parents no longer have a world to themselves, or they have to vigorously reclaim it.

Oliva Newton-John interrupts my daydreams: "At least there's some life in your shack. We constantly start arguing from sheer boredom."

I reply: "I'm not the kinda guy who needs life around him." Seriously. I love to stare out of the window. To watch how nothing is happening at all and then I'm happy about gawking and the only thing you've got to do is wave at your fellow gawkers to ignore them again afterward."

I don't think the unemployed animal lover understands what I'm saying. "Our new neighbor livened up our shack a bit. At night, heavy bangs make us jump out of bed. She listens to Bavarian brass music on full blast and bangs her doors. That was a completely different story when you guys were still there."

I can't imagine that the next tenant bangs doors to brass music. It's more likely that she smacks her calves or chops wood with an ax.

And well, the 'peace and quiet'. As soon as Finn was born, Olivia and Riccardo swapped their bedroom with the guest room for distance reasons. And how many nights we could hear somebody roaring from the apartment below ours: "Quiet, damn it!"

The mutt almost climbed into the stroller at this point. Finn is feeding her with his pacifier chain. Oliva Newton-John takes a new cigarette out of the pack while I've got comfortable on my bicycle seat.

Then Carla and Steffen come around the corner. Susanne told me that Carla is finally pregnant, but I would have noticed it anyway. During pregnancy, when the puking phase eventually disappears beyond the horizon, just before the panicky nest-building syndrome rises, pregnant women have a look of boundless mercy. Even Carla. Usually, you could describe her as quite stern, like her hair that is tightly tied back. No excuses and she reminds me of Therese Giese, just a bit more fierce and severe. But not now. She's floating along the sidewalk, glowing with inner bliss.

I think to myself, Don't say anything wrong now.

For example: "Just wait for the hormonal reversal to set in shortly after birth." Poor Steffen will be for the high jump, and her hair will be pulled back more tightly than ever.

"Hello, you two." Both are all smiles.

I've never seen the two of them beaming like this before. They usually stick to arguing. Outright and mean arguing. Even at their wedding, he barked at her, and she at him. Although Carla's mother is quite warm and kind, or maybe because of that.

I don't know. Somehow this seems to be the common level of communication. Steffen is usually pretty quiet when he's not arguing with Carla.

"I heard you want to open a practice on the expected date of delivery," I say to Carla. She grins. "My goodness, that's going to be exhausting," I continue, and I'm about to lose my good intentions. In a few minutes, I'm going to bring them back down to earth with my embellished horror stories about birth.

"Tell me, what has actually changed since your son was born?" Steffen asks cautiously.

"Well, I'll tell you one thing right away: it's not going to make the relationship any better!" Silence. Even Olivia Newton-John, who is now playing with the pacifier chain instead of the mutt, looks up in surprise.

"Well, that sounds like fun," Steffen replies, sounding slightly intimidated. And I think: Does that count as cattiness? I'd have to ask my older brother whether such forms of being mean even exist.

All my dams of silence are broken now:

"Two weeks after giving birth, Susanne chased me to the mall for emergency shopping after not sleeping at all, with no time to brush my teeth and in barely any clothes. I was supposed to get a red-light lamp, a bottle warmer, and some homeopathic globules to calm the nerves.

I stood in front of three IR lamps and a sales-woman. She insisted that I had to tell her what I wanted to use it for; otherwise, she could not help me. Was I supposed to say: 'The screaming blood-thirsty and neckless monster sucked Mom's nipples bloody to see if it can squeeze out another drop?' I opted for the cheapest model, despite the warning of the shopping specialist.

'I warned you,' I could hear her scolding me while still at the shelf with the bottle warmers, and, 'You will need a sanitizer device, too. Everyone who buys a bottle warmer needs that.' All around me, I could hear children screaming, and I took the bottle warmer with the fewest applications.

Back home, we had a visitor: Susanne's boss with her boyfriend and children. The boss's boss wouldn't shut up about her own birth and her tattered femininity and some sauce dripping out of her, and I was hungry for breakfast.

After looking at the premises, the child, and the gifts, and some inevitable advice, the visiting boss made her way home. But I was ordered to very quickly rush to the curly head in the pharmacy to get an emergency pack of dry food in case the breasts would refuse to serve. I had breakfast, lunch, and dinner at the same time, standing up or already lying down. I can't remember."

I talk and talk. The scraggy one and Granny Gröllbeck from the window are also listening in now, more or less captivated.

"Or would you like to hear the story about how Suanne's mother 'Klärchen' first came to visit? I'm telling you 'exasperating'. After sweet gifts and more inevitable advice, Klärchen came up with a problem-solving approach, even though she was still wearing her coat from the trip: 'You have to powder the child. Then it won't scream anymore.' After that, Susanne and her mother got into an argument. I'm telling you, what an ordeal."

The mutt is asleep, Granny Gröllbeck at the window is waving her fly swatter: "We all had to go through that. That's the first three months for you. My Bernd was very irascible too."

Oh, I think, her Bernd is our janitor today. Really, he's our former janitor and certainly nothing less problematic than in the first three months of his life. When he's not drunk, he's pretty aggressive, and I'm sure his daughter Olivia didn't have an easy time with Granny Gröllbeck's Bernd.

Last year, Granny and granddaughter Gröllbeck stood waving at the intersection of Alt-Moabit and Paulstraße and cryingly gestured him into the opposite building, to be exact, into cell 283 of the opposite building.

The mutt and Finn dozed off. Steffen yawns, even though the sleepless nights still lie ahead of him. Carla must be dreaming of nursery decorations, Olivia Newton-John of a new snake for the terrarium, and Dad listens to his own captivating stories:

"... and Finn's first birthday. I'm telling you, the blaring of four children and their mothers, who could talk for hours over Sacher cake about the texture of what their offspring leaves in their diapers: 'I'm not sure if I should go to the doctor. The little one always poops this greenish-gray stuff now. It's almost bluish. And I don't know if it's not a tad too thin. I think a specialist needs to look at it.'

Finn was a little stressed out on his big day because he had to endure one full hour of baby swimming with his Mom in the morning and then another hour of touching and swaying in the baby group. At some point, the moms dropped all inhibitions and restraints: Somebody played a video from their last PEKiP class, in real-time, mind you. At the same time, Helen was playing 'Sur le pont, d'Ávignon on the flute; Susanne showed Kerstin photos of what Finn looked like a week ago, calming the latter by playing the hopper wagon game with him.

Henry forced a tongue kiss on another child, which possibly escalated into a tongue bite. I couldn't see what happened exactly because I was pushed to look at some embryonic ultrasound recordings. Then, the part of the video started, in which all mothers sing 'Ticke Tacke Ticke Tacke' while squatting in a circle on something ecological..."

The scraggy one, who doesn't have any children, puts some treats from the bakery in front of the mutt's snout. The mutt is asleep. Yawning, Granny Gröllbeck chases away pigeons with her swatter. Carla has to sit on the bench in front of the bakery and take a deep breath.

But Dad has no time to catch his breath: "... and he calls me 'mommy' all the time to get me back for the spiteful stories. Even though I've always told him that there is only 'the boss' and 'the chief' for him. I mean, he can say things like 'aqua' and 'woof woof', and they are pretty difficult...".

"For us, it's not any better. Saskia is having a hard time, too. She's got issues with her medial meniscus," Olivia Newton interrupts. "If the injections don't help, then..." She runs her fingers across her throat, demonstratively dangling her tongue out.

"Shouldn't you get a stroller with three wheels to ride more comfortably?" objects Dr. Steffen.

"... And it's pricey. Each jab 25 euros. And all that from our benefits. Tough times. I'd like to start cutting salaries at the very top ...," Olivia grumbles, tugging vigorously at her jacket.

"Oh, don't come at me with that equipment. It's all cheap, poorly fabricated stuff. And unreasonably overpriced," I retort to whoever.

"What kind of breed is that? A Black Retriever?" the scraggy one wants to know.

"Even putting him to down costs 30 euros? Mix of Italian olive dog with something German" snorts Oliva.

At some point, Olivia Newton-John entertains the scraggy one about the injustice of the world. Steffen argues with Carla about if strollers should have three or four wheels. Granny Gröllbeck talks to the woman in the other window about her son Bernd and how cute he once was. Finn is awake and demonstratively stiffens up in his stroller to make everybody aware to please focus their attention on him, and I talk into the void for a few more minutes.

Chapter 6

We, the bike, the stroller, including contents, and Dad, push pretty much directly home. The 'pretty much' means nothing other than Dad trying to hopefully avoid all the playgrounds and other time-consuming obstacles on the route.

The thought is barely finished when a squadron of pigeons lands directly in our entry lane. After throwing all rules of conduct overboard, the golden little mouse struts apparently willingly after these critters. As if by a magnetically attracted, remote-controlled, programmed bird-following instinct. Only by doing some spurting and Finn doing some loud screaming can we continue after towards our last goal.

I suspect that the cause of this conditioning is his Mom and her belief that children always need to be around animals. Whether on the children's farm, in the apartment, in picture books, or elsewhere: "Look, Finn, quick! A tweet-tweet" or "Listen, there must be a woof-woof close by". Or Susanne grunts like a pig or says: "Dad's going to do the goose now". Then I, a reasonably cultivated Central European, have to cackle 'goh-goh-goh-goh' on the spot.

Fire engines hold a similar fascination. Especially the ones with big ladders. And they have to be loud, fast and red. For Finn, standing in front of the gates of the Wiener Strasse fire station is the equivalent of at least a dozen pigeons landing in front of him. Either the gate opens, and something shoots out, or a fire truck returns. Better, of course, is shooting off.

That leaves the playgrounds, but I think they're boring: sliding-climbing-swinging-sliding-climbing-swinging. And then the whole thing all over again. And no matter when I say it's time for us to go, the child throws a nice temper tantrum and would prefer to slide, or swing, or climb one more time. That's why I know these obstacles on our route oh so well, and don't say no to a small detour if we arrive home a lot sooner.

The pigeons are out of sight. Finn takes his usual position in his stroller with one foot hanging casually out to the side. His whole body is crookedly sprawled in the cart most of the time, and sometimes the head dangles out somewhere.

In front of my inner eye, I can see Finn's future driving style pretty clearly: one hand loosely flapping out of the car window, the other on the steering wheel, or grabbing the chick. But maybe he just doesn't really like this stroller model or the lambskin inside.

Now I understand why the stupid sheep on the children's farm always bleat at the stroller: they recognize their flattened fellow, or better, what is left of him. No doubt.

Finn shouldn't have any problems with the fellow: he is conditioned to animals and everything animal-like. Especially since this piece of lamb also lay under his pregnant Mom and was soaked in sweat at night together with Mrs. Hansen. And that was a sweltering summer back then. It can't really be the color of the stroller either: mouse gray slightly fading into dusty blue.

That leaves only the inflatable off-road tires. Although this is less of a necessity in Kreuzberg, the dog shit sticks to the profile quite nicely and can only be removed with some effort. Thinking about it, Finn developed a technique to fumble off the biggest chunks while driving. To do so, you have to lay crosswise in the cart.

Right before we get to the house, just behind the substation, we can see the last two unavoidable obstacles: the pack of seagulls on the Landwehr Canal bridge and the sandbox in the beer garden, exactly three stories below our apartment.

The pack of seagulls is more of a hurdle for me. Countless, and in my opinion, quite hefty specimens like to get much too close to me. I will be careful not to feed them. They would only mobilize their relatives from all roofs to threaten me as well.

Finn observes the Hitchcock bird attack for a few minutes while disinterestedly sucking on his pretzel before pointing to the sandbox in the beer garden with a vehement "doh".

If I owned a beer garden like that directly at the water, I would undoubtedly cram every free spot with tables and chairs. This owner is different: He decided on a pretty large sandbox with lots of molds to argue about and even more space around it.

By now, I understand this marketing campaign a little better. At the crack of dawn – all the other cafés are still yawning with a lack of guests – three floors below us, the entire squadron of neighboring parents, including their offspring, is gathered around and inside the sandbox and the latte macchiato. Late in the evening, when this target group collectively and lethargically falls into bed, a wooden board is placed on top of the box and the DINK (Double-Income-No-Kids) target group comes together in their cozy lounge area. Brilliant, isn't it? Unfortunately, it's not so brilliant for us who live above. When are you actually supposed to get your well-deserved night's rest? Mrs. Bollmann, one floor below, complains about too much noise from time to time.

We don't care as Finn keeps us awake at night frequently and for a long time anyway. Sleeping well is something I did 16 months ago. No, it was actually over even a few months before that, thanks to the pregnant woman constantly stomping to the toilet or permanently snoring.

I remember a phone call with my older sister sometime during the pregnancy:

"What do you want for your birthday?" she asked me.

"I've seen this alarm clock that is actually absolutely silent. I have such a hard time falling asleep with the ticking."

My sister only laughed, and I had a hard time calming her down. Running toddler groups and having two children of her own, she didn't believe that a ticking alarm clock, of all things, would keep me from sleeping in the future.

She was proven to be correct.

Dad doesn't feel like enjoying the sandbox and definitely the squadron of parents squatting there. So, I distract the golden darling by flooding him with words like: "Ladder, screwdriver, and imagine a dowel…" Finn looks at me curiously as I pull him past the entrance. "… and a drill even, on the ladder!"

He is completely overwhelmed. Objects of that type mean unspeakable happiness to him. Just naming these objects stops him from all planned actions. His face says: Where? When are they coming? Susanne makes use of those expressions in the car. They always keep him from falling asleep for some time.

I managed to creep past the danger zone, past the entire front yard along with the stroller and bike. The front door is open. Now, all that's left to do is get the bike into the basement and unpack the load inside.

Finn is dragged out of the stroller. He probably expects to see the enlightenment behind the basement door in the form of a dowel or screwdriver. He's on the right, the bicycle on the left, in front of us, I read the sign: "It's not allowed to enter the basement with a light or lamp but only with a closed lantern".

Finn is the one hitting the light switch. In the process, he pulls a handful of spiderwebs in my face adding the comment "Doh".

In the meantime, I have turned on the light, and I'm trying to drag the objects down the very narrow basement stairs with the greatest effort. The bike always gets wedged just before reaching the basement corridor. Finn comments this by imitating a groan even before I get the chance to moan myself. I have to grin despite the load and then groan even grouchier.

Once downstairs, the little woodlouse immediately shows me the way to our basement room. As the house has never been renovated properly, you can still see residues of charcoal and dust on the basement floor. But there is no way around it. To unlock our room, I have to put Finn and the bike down. "Where the hell is the key?" I ask into the semi-dark vault.

Finn replies, "Doh," pointing his black grimy fingers at the lock on the door. I unlock it, and Finn starts crawling into the dark paradise.

"Stop, first the bike and then the dirty little rag," Dad coughs absentmindedly.

What can I do? I can't leave him alone in the yard upstairs. He might eat the garbage or at least rearrange the flower beds to his liking. Now in the evening, it doesn't really matter. But in the morning? And then to the kindergarten? Heike looked punitively at Finn's hands and pants just last week. But the grime was more persistent than her gaze despite subsequent knocking and washing on my part.

"Is someone there?" I hear a voice from above. "Can I lock up, hello?"

"No, don't!" I reply, "We're down here."

I think I recognize Mrs. Bollmann's voice: "Oh, I thought someone forgot about the cellar door again. Wouldn't be the first time." Mrs. Bollmann is a bit snippy in her verbal phrasing. About 50 years old. Quite solitary but not in the sense of lonely, I think, more out of conviction.

We only got this apartment here at the Paul-Lincke-Ufer under the condition to talk to Bollmann first, as she apparently doesn't care for a family to live directly above her. Susanne and I could understand that very well. The former tenant was usually away, inhabited a maximum of two rooms, and had no TV or other noisemakers. I wouldn't really look forward to three screaming, excessively moving, and around-the-clock bustling creatures moving in above my home.

Susanne called her at that time, saying: "So, you don't like children?

But Ms. Bollmann didn't want to be put in this children-hater pigeonhole. Even back then, I thought Susanne was clever. Since then, she has used every opportunity to teasingly tug at the little bugger pretending to be interested. The little bugger and we don't really believe her – the part of being interested. But she is actually quite lovely and just a little snippy and curious. As soon as we had entered the new apartment for the first time, even before it got renovated, she rang the doorbell.

"I wanted to take a look at the apartment and see how it's laid out."

I was suspicious she actually wanted to take a look at us. We did pretty well, as she stayed longer than expected, and we had to look at her apartment posthaste. It was laid out identically. Everything was fully renovated and spick and span clean. At the same time, our apartment was in the condition of something that had been rarely inhabited for the past 38 years and even less often renovated.

I towed myself and the little chimney sweep back up to daylight. Mrs. Bollmann has already positioned herself there to have a little chat.

"Be careful, Mrs. Bollmann. Finn has chickenpox. Don't catch it. We've just come from the doctor's," I warn her as Finn runs over to his tricycle and the bicycles.

"Oh, poor little guy. He's going to have a hard time sleeping tonight," she replies. I think she means that she herself will probably sleep worse thanks to the noise.

I notice a sign in the yard. "Children playing in the yard, hallway and stairs, and standing around outside the front door is strictly prohibited" Interesting, these signs around here, I think. You need a closed lantern for the basement, and you can't just stand around – strictly prohibited. The little grimy mouse is now examining an oily bicycle chain for its elasticity.

"He doesn't look sick at all. He looks more like he fell down a chimney," she continues. I turn around to Finn and watch him rubbing his grime-oil hands across his face. No, actually more extensive. Also, all over his hair and down to the neck and back up to the nose.

"Are you out of your mind, Finn?" Dad yells. Finn knocks the bike over – he seems to be getting cranky. It's time for us to end this chat before he really gets going: "We have to ...", I reply to Mrs. Bollmann and grab the grimy-oil buck.

On the way up to the third floor, he tries a few more times successfully to knock my sunglasses off my head and onto the floor, despite or because of my screaming as I bend down to grab them.

I unlock the door and heave us inside. "Stop, little sport. First, take off your shoes, wash your hands and go to the box for a diaper change."

It seems as if he didn't understand me, as he immediately hops underneath the stretched swing into the study to the bookshelf. "No, not like that!" I call after him, but unfortunately have to make a detour via the hallway and the dining room and a gigantic fire truck – never seen that before.

Finn is coming toward me holding a book: The Mormon Bible. The things we own. I sit down on the floor and look at the book. This can't be mine, but then who else could have brought this home?

Finn gets back with two more books and sits down close to me. He is browsing in "Coming into the World". I am still engaged with the Mormon Bible.

Oh, what's the other book he has there? My "The Loneliness of the Long Distance Runner." I put the Mormon book away and take the long-distance runner. Finn is on page nine now: "...meanwhile, the semen slept with millions of semen in my father's testicles."

I don't know if that's a good choice for a 1 1/2-year-old. He seems to like it, though, at least turning the pages. I'm looking forward to flipping through the long-distance runner, which I've read at least 20 times. A thrill each and every time. But then, it's only 55 pages. At least it's in English. Finn is now at conception." ...meanwhile, in my mom's belly, the egg was about to leave..."

What books we have. Certainly not mine. "That's enough," I mumble as I put all three books back on the shelf. Half of its contents are on the floor. Finn grabs another book: "The Practice of Tooth Removal."

"Take off your shoes, wash your hands, I'll change your diapers!" and I drag him into the bathroom. Turning on the faucet, putting the stool in front of him, lifting the child up, and rubbing him. The grime comes off easier than the oil. Once on the changing table, Finn is still holding his "The Practice of Tooth Removal" and has by now reached the chapter: "Removing the bone, including incision".

Mommy has placed a few cuddly objects around his changing spot: Schorschi, a promotional gift from the Bausparkasse is supposed to be a fox, next to it a poison-green bear with the scarf imprint 'Skoda'. At the top is a bed bottle cover in the shape of a sheep. Next to it polar bears, other lambs, and an Ernie. Barely any room for the child.

He couldn't care less about these figures: 'Wound care after surgical tooth removal' seems much more interesting.

I tear off the old diaper and take a new one, a good one, from the package. Shortly after birth, the "not yet arrived" darling was always wet through. We didn't know if he was just sweating a lot or if we unprofessionally put on his diaper. I was close to contacting Mr. Pampers to complain about a faulty product. It always looks much drier in the commercials. We eventually came to terms with it – the leakage, I mean. We actually found a manufacturer who keeps his promises and stays fix. Everything else will sooner or later be completely soaked.

Finn has had it and cries. Took too long, the wrong diaper brand after all, not enough new things in the tooth pulling book – no idea. But I really can't bear the screaming after this exhausting afternoon.

"We'll take a bath now," I say, and my Finn gets into his tub. Fixies off again, putting the little rascal on the floor, and he waddles off to the bath.

Bathing is as good for crying as chocolate is for teeth. Even as a newborn, his Mom took him to the baby swimming class. He loved the water, but the collective obligation to dive in he particularly despised. To this day, he doesn't like water on his face or his face underwater.

He's grouching in front of the tub, and out of sheer anticipation, he decides to pee on the bathroom carpet. I stare at the ceiling.

He says, "Ahh."
I say, "Is that really necessary?"
He says, "Ahh."
Well, hopefully, by the time the boss comes home, the stain will be dry. He throws the entire repertoire of squeaky ducks, along with an Ernie cup, five empty yogurt cups, Mom's shampoo, his toothbrush, the monster plug on the floor, and the tooth book into the tub. I fish some of it back out, especially Mom's reference book against teeth, while Finn is trying to chuck other things in: the toilet roll, his towel, and the big fire truck.

"That's it, you little water rat. You won't fit in the tub." I help him get in. He squats down and is excited. I take the towel stroking his face with the wet rag.

Finn stands up, points to the bear costume, and wants out now. Too much water in too many facial areas.

"Oh no, sit back down." Nothing you can do.

He screams and tries to climb out. I gently squat him down into the water. He's decided enough is enough. Too bad, really. Changing into the bear costume, walking over to Finn's room on the changing table, turning the hairdryer on, and the screaming is over. The boss won't like the grime-oil mix on his hand. I rub his hands for a while, skillfully distracting him with the hairdryer.

The phone rings. Great. Perfect timing. I drag him to the floor – without any clothes – and run to the phone.

Ria, the 'Sur le Pont D'Avignon'-woman, needs advice ASAP: Her grayish-blue pooping Henry – or was that the French kissing one? – has no appetite and is screaming less than usual.

"Ria, what am I supposed to do now?"

"Where's Susanne?" she asks frantically.

"She doesn't get off work before 8:00. But don't worry about it. There's always the emergency service on Graefestraße if his symptoms get worse," I reassure her as I continue soothing Finn with the hairdryer on the floor.

"Is it possible that Henry has an ear infection?" she asks.

"I don't think so. Don't they usually have a fever in that case?", I smartass at her. Finn arches his back like a cat and visibly enjoys the blowing of the hairdryer. However, it's not so easy for me to reach him anymore now. He sort of worms under his bed, and I wave after him with the machine – while holding the other machine to my ear.

"Guess what, Finn has chickenpox. We just came from the doctor."

"No, he certainly got that in his kindergarten..." concludes Ria, who's been busy for weeks and weeks, carefully selecting a nanny for her golden darling from a multitude of applicants. She shares an architect's office with Werner and needs more time for the bad times and the office.

"... I've had one job interview after another today. Not very satisfying, though. None has really met my requirement profile. Hopefully, Henry didn't catch it from any of the candidates..."

Listening to Ria halfheartedly, I try to put the arching cat in diapers and tights.

Pretty tricky with one hand.

"You never know what they bring into your house. 12 applicants and not one that I would take right off the bat..."

Ever since her little mischief-maker was born, Ria has been quite concerned. I remember our first 'get-together'. Susanne knew her from one of many pregnancy classes, and not only Ria. I was introduced to a seemingly never-ending network of mothers.

After the birth, sometime in December, I was supposed to participate together with other couples in a collective Sunday stroller-pushing towards Treptower Park.

My mood was as low as it gets, and in an act of protesting, I dyed my hair red and yellow one hour before the date the boss had set for us. Poorly motivated and uncommunicative, the red and yellow Dad pushed the stroller around a few blocks in lockstep with the other people present in the freezing cold. Like a promenading "We are the pushing stroller protest", including a sour Dad.

Leonhard's stroller was, of course, all black without any applications – or anything really – as well as his Triptrap children's chair and everything else later on. Just black. And you couldn't recognize him at all. Wrapped in way too many clothes.

The protest ended in Ria's and Werner's apartment in the Schlesische Straße with an unspectacular round of coffee.

Sometime later, under more positive circumstances, I found them both to be quite entertaining. For example, when we spent last New Year's Eve with them eating raclette. No, not until midnight. Maybe until 8 pm. At that point, for the hosts and for us New Year's Eve was over – or did we actually stay up until midnight when we got home? I can't remember. Anyway, Finn threw a nice screaming fit just in time for the toast at midnight.

The two architects also invited us to a party – I think they called it an 'event'. This happened at Fischers Fritz, right next to the Universal Music building. The food would certainly have been delicious. Unfortunately, I had to drop the spoon before the 1st course because Mom and Dad had forgotten the formula for Finn's bottle.

I was crossing the Oberbaumbrücke to go back home with my beige jacket. When I arrived back there, the 2nd course was served. But first, the starving and screaming little darling had to be calmed down. After all of his sucking about, the plan was for him to rest and fall asleep.

But apparently, there was not a single room in the whole building where you could deposit him and his stroller. So, I had to go outside and look for a quiet spot on the banks of the Spree.

As luck would have it, a techno parade was happening in Berlin that same day, and there simply was no quiet spot. One booming boat after another was banging acoustically into the stroller.

One raver advised me to try the whole thing at the Stralauer Allee. This main road makes a constant monotonous noise, and that would have worked for him, too. Dad pushed the tired cargo at the rim of the never-ending and continuously loud traffic noises.

In contrast to the raver, Finn perceived that quite differently. Indeed, the latter was short a few doses of Ecstasy to absorb the consonance of the buzzing cars in a way that would stimulate his sleep. Without fulfilling my deed, I went back to Fischers Fritz. Susanne took the cart and tried to wiggle the child to sleep in the bathroom. Too bad that the meal was interrupted by one and speech after the other.

Mom had little success. I could hear that even from my seat. We left pretty exhaustedly before the dessert.

Ria told me the next day that the party went on until 5 am. Our party went on at home until about 1 in the morning. Then on at 3 and again at half-past five.

There was a fellow networker worth mentioning, but I can't remember her name now. Immediately after the birth, still in the hospital, we met in the hallway with the little baby carriage and the newborns.

I said to her: "We are not so lucky. Ours turned out quite ugly. He looks like my father, only at least 20 years older."

"Well, take a look in my carriage. Neither I nor Christian look like that kid. Like a monkey. Compared to that, yours is quite cute. Ours is a gorilla. And how big he is already."

I thought it to be open-hearted at the time. And unusual for the mother species. She immediately went back to work as a lawyer. Unfortunately, we're no longer in contact with her. It didn't really fit, I guess. We invited her to an Easter brunch. After that, it was over. Maybe it was because ... Well, I'd better leave it at that.

Katie is also part of the mom's network. I think she works as a lawyer too, but what's worse, she's pregnant again.

One time Finn was, I think, quite mean to her and her Leon. They came to visit. Finn had no intention to share just one of his toys that day. Leon got nothing, nothing at all. Our sweet child was alone in his room for quite some time, which he never did voluntarily. Suddenly he came to us and pushed poor Katie to the front door.

In disbelief, she said, "He doesn't mean us, does he? Is he kicking us out?"

I said nothing and grinned secretly to myself. Finn was quite serious. He wasn't up for network meetings that day. And the mostly apathetic Leon and Katie left soon. For better or worse.

"...maybe the Croatian? Although she doesn't know any German. That's not good for Henry's language development. But otherwise, she is quite ingenious ..." Ria rattles on. "...I signed him up for a music school. I think that's very important..."

Dad says nothing, but maybe she should try to persuade him to walk first. All Henry does is strange hopping. It's true that this hop technique is extremely sophisticated. Still, this child can't spend his entire life bouncing around with his legs crossed holding a recorder. Well, that's none of this Dad's business. There's someone else for that: Werner. Since the birth of his son, he spends much more time at the office. And in other respects, too, Ria has absolutely free reigns in terms of bringing up their child.

"...How are you doing with the new apartment? All the boxes unpacked yet?", Ria asks dead on target. No matter what I reply now, she's about to do her professional canvassing act.

"Well, if we keep consuming like this, we'll soon need an even bigger apartment," I reply.

"Buying is just the thing for you. I've already told you about our project..."

Finn has scuffled into the balcony room, where he is safely occupied with his wooden train set.

"...You'd only need 20% equity. And I'm telling you, the project is amazing. And don't' get me started about the location..."

I'm not really listening to her anymore. After all, I explained to her a few weeks ago that we won't buy any apartment in our current situation. Who knows where we'll be in a year or two? Maybe somewhere completely different.

"...that would only be a monthly burden of 825 €..." I can't hear any more wooden train noises and decide to have a look. "Ahh, stop, Ria. I have to hang up. Finn's just making a big mess." Dad puts the phone down and sees how the little darling is massaging the potting soil from the yucca plant nice and evenly into the duvet.

"Have you gone nuts? How am I supposed to get that out of the bedding? We'll need the vacuum cleaner first, darn it."

Finn is happy – probably because there is finally something going on again. Not as dull as the last couple of minutes. He's already in the pantry, rattling the vacuum cleaner pole.

It turns out the idea with the vacuum cleaner wasn't really that great. Using the apparatus is smearing the dirt across the linen more than vacuuming it. Finn enjoys it so much that he quickly throws a handful of dirt on the bed. "That's enough – I had enough, you monster."

As soon as I have stripped the beds and put Finn into his pajamas, the Mom shows up. Without taking off her jacket and shoes, she rushes straight to her little ray of sunshine, purring, "You poor sick little darling."

I remove myself – no, too soon. I have to clean the bathroom first and then prepare Finn's bottle and bed for the night.

Mom is squatting with him in front of a picture book: "My animals on the farm. I only hear baaing, grunting, and cackling from next door.

When all is done, I come back and hand over the milk bottle, Mrs. Hansen, and the dummy to the boss. Finn is sucking while meditatively fiddling with Hansen's string. Susanne tells me about a difficult tooth extraction. If she only knew that her book is drying on the balcony and earlier, her son was plowing through several chapters.

Dad talks about his exhausting afternoon with the kids, but Mom is already singing: "Sleep, little child, sleep. Father tends the sheep."

I get kicked in the hip as an unmistakable sign to sing along and accompany the night express to bed.

I sing: "...the father is the sheep, the boss is the herd animal, watch out she won't smack you diagonal, sleep little child, sleep." I slip away, get something alcoholic, and sit down in front of the TV.

Before 9 pm, I'm in bed. The phone rings next door. Surely the network. I hear Susanne yawning continuously. That can only be Klärchen, and I fall asleep.

Appendix

The chickenpox phase was reasonably tolerable. Oh, one night, there actually was a break-in in the new apartment. A few of Finn's toys have gone missing: the laptop, the drill, and the TV now have children of other parents to play with. Although my sleep is so light and all the doors, including the one with the swing, were open, and Finn woke up every hour thanks to his chickenpox, we didn't hear anything from the burglars. Luckily.

Unfortunately, the detective who was looking for clues afterward left his little hammer unattended in the kitchen: our golden darling, the sweet little boy, used the time while I went to the bathroom for literally 10 seconds in the best way possible: he grabbed the little hammer packed, gave the newly purchased Siemen's laundry machine a little hack and disassembled the glass of the bull's eye professionally into tiny portions.

Customer service advises us to buy a new one, because of the replacement being quite expensive.

During our chickenpox afternoon, we forever said goodbye to the pilot from the wooden airplane, the dummy chain with the red cows, and the left shoe. None of the listed exhibits have reappeared to this day.

In the meantime, we spent the Easter holidays in a well-organized way. One of the highlights was visiting the Volkswagen dealership. They had Easter eggs for children to paint.

Mom was sitting there at a booth crafting an egg for half an eternity. Finn was busy at first running after a two-meter-tall Easter bunny hoping that he would give him a chocolate egg for the umpteenth time. Later, he was only interested in the decoration or the removal of the same.

For some time, I was standing in front of a pile of huddled-up cottontails. Later, Susanne picked up some brochures about a particularly ugly model of the Passat – as a Variant, of course. This car dealership hopping is quite popular at the moment. Unfortunately, we haven't visited the "DaimlerChrysler" highlight yet. The network said this one is a paradise for our little rascals.

Heike from daycare didn't wear her glasses one morning. When I asked her, she said, "I forgot them in the bedroom, and I didn't want to wake my husband up."

Since that time, I have never seen her with her glasses again. Strange, isn't it? Has her husband been sleeping for two weeks straight, and she can't get her glasses?

But instead, her colleague, Christine, who never wore glasses, has a pair now. Office manager model with a matt black horn frame. Also, her hair glows orange instead of brown now. Courageous, I think. Heike also changed her hair, but as I said, I don't pay attention to her hairstyle.

In the meantime, Dagmar mailed me "Hope": "According to the Göttingen neurobiologist Prof. Dr. Gerald Hüther, only relatively few people find happiness because almost all of them stick to looking at the wrong places. For example, a life without problems is not at all desirable because overcoming difficulties makes you happy and promotes an optimistic outlook on life."

I continue to try to overcome and do my best. But why on earth did no one warn me, dear parents and dear friends?

Continued Appendix

... Stuffed to the gills, we drive on the city highway towards the airport – it's better to get into a traffic jam right before the airport. Dad squeezed tightly behind the wheel because Finn insists on his legroom in the back seat. After all, it wasn't him who chose this cramped little car. Whenever the driver's seat is too far back, Finn's feet are constantly rammed into the upholstery using his vocal cords to fervently support this action. Well, close to the steering wheel, it is.

Next to me, virtually as a passenger, sits a travel bag, a backpack, and a brochure with the title "Dental Office Kit for upper and lower jaws". Oh yeah, and the brochure "Patent Kit in tubes and syringes" is under the backpack. I can already see myself sitting on the plane later with these documents and Susanne having difficulty talking the patient into bleaching her teeth.

"I'll put the documents in the back, yeah!", I mutter into the rearview mirror. Susanne, sitting in the back next to her golden darling, doesn't react, and I yawn apathetically in the direction of the airport's main hall. We've been standing in the same spot for 30 minutes – about 500 meters outside the terminal. The brochures remain my passengers.

"I miss you already," I can hear a sad whisper from behind. The backpack, the giant bag, and the brochures do not respond. Dad answers: "If this goes on like this, or actually stands on like this, you don't have to worry about that. But we're still fairly good on time."

That's no surprise. Finn didn't sleep very well that night – but was rested a little earlier than usual. That's why we were ready to leave at the crack of dawn.

Somehow, the airport's main hall seems to magnetically attract its fellow travelers, as it happens more and more often that next to, behind, or in front of us, a car door is frantically yanked open, and a briefcase along with its owner is hurled out of the car toward the airport. Almost like those electric fly-killing UV lamps, this building seems to have an inescapable attraction. The only thing missing is the sizzling noise when they reach the entrance door.

"Maybe we should start walking, too, Finni-baby," I comment on the frantic they-won't-catch-their-flight-activity outside our stress-free zone. We still have almost three hours left to start our 50-minute journey.